How to Catch a Leprechaun

Published by Sourcebooks Jabberwocky, an imprint of Sourcebooks, Inc.
P.O. Box 4410, Naperville, Illinois 60567-4410
(630) 961-3900
Fax: (630) 961-2168
www.jabberwockykids.com

The Library of Congress Cataloging-in-Publication data is on file with the publisher.

Source of Production: Shenzhen Wing King Tong Paper Products Co. Ltd., Longgang District, Shenzhen, China
Date of Production: September 2019
Run Number: 5016207

Printed and bound in China.
WKT 12

How to Catch a Leprechaun

Words by Adam Wallace

Pictures by Andy Elkerton

sourcebooks
jabberwocky

The night is dark, the streets are quiet,
ST. PATRICK'S DAY is near.
I tap my hammer so you'll know
the Leprechaun is here!

I'll pull out all your laces,
put GLITTER
in your hair.

And when you walk around, you'll see
my GOLD coins everywhere.

You'll never catch me in your trap,
    but, yes, I'll make a scene!
I'll turn the whole place upside down.
    Your toilet will be green!

House number one.

I'm going in!

Really? That's your trap?

I'm in and out, without a doubt.
That one was a SNAP!

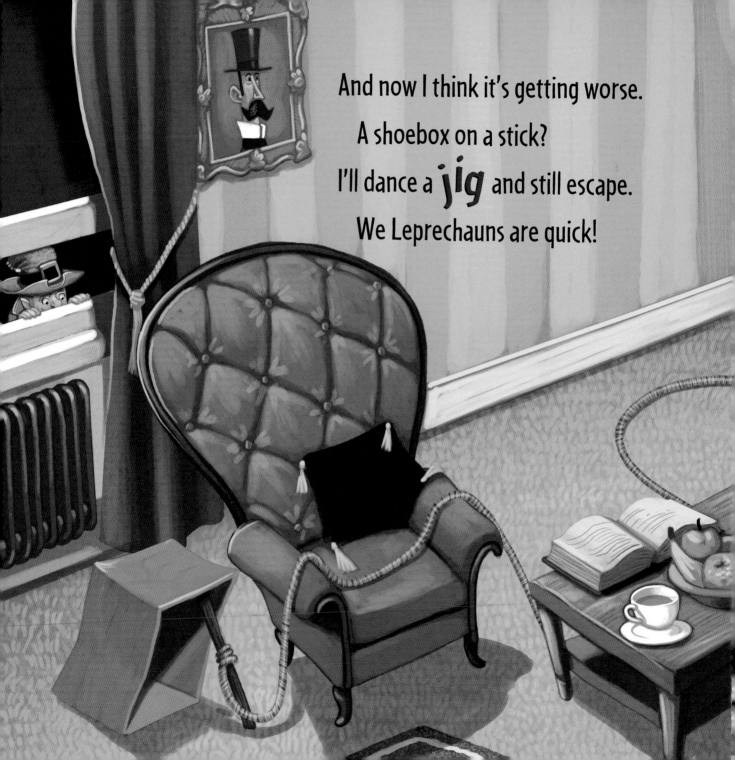

And now I think it's getting worse.
A shoebox on a stick?
I'll dance a **jig** and still escape.
We Leprechauns are quick!

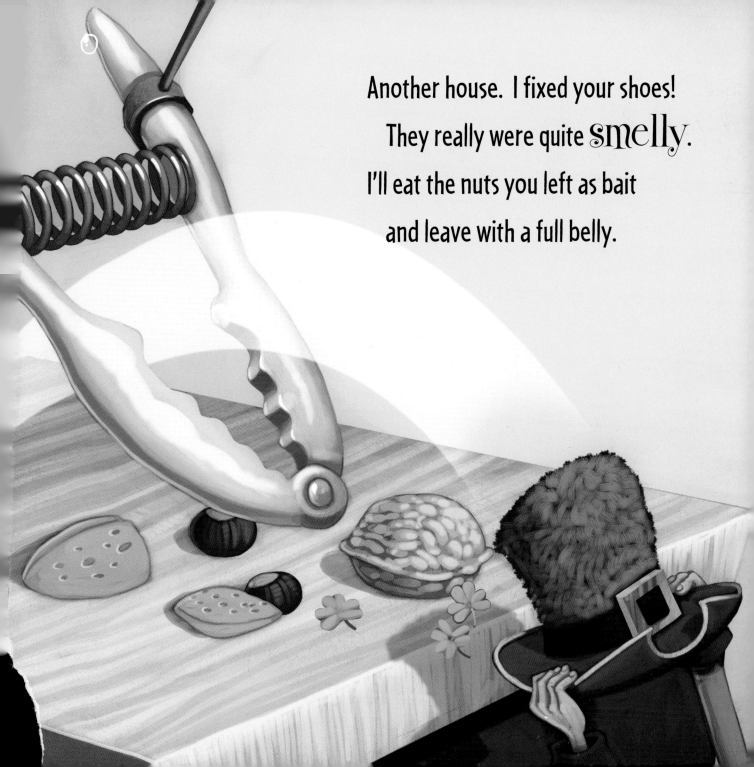

Another house. I fixed your shoes!
They really were quite smelly.
I'll eat the nuts you left as bait
and leave with a full belly.

Now you're talking! Look at this.
It's **dandelion tea!**
But I'm too speedy for your trap.
This tea is mine for free!

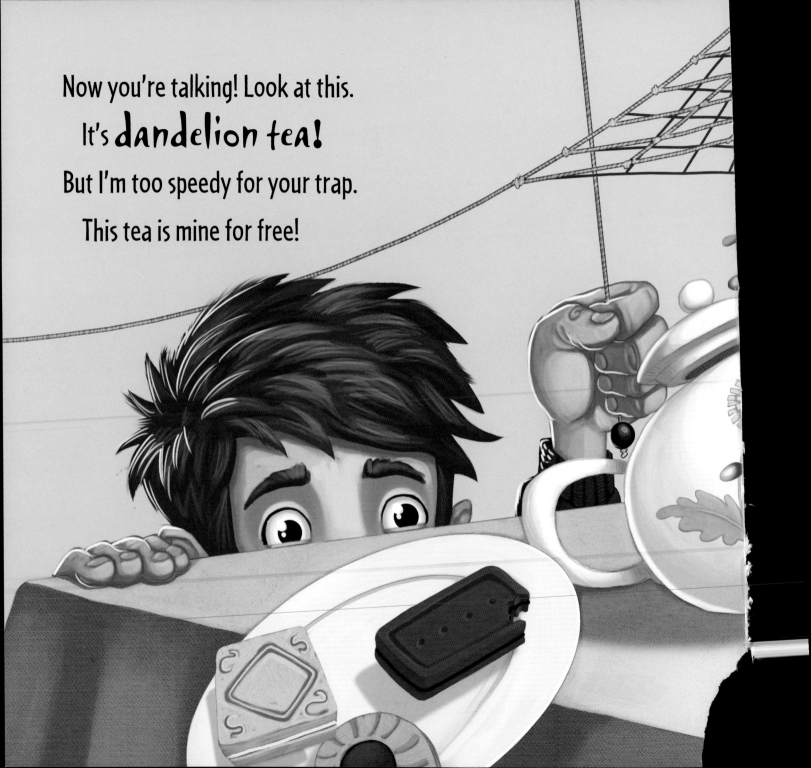

I know you want my pot of gold.
That **IRON CAGE** was clever.
But I've been alive 200 years.
You won't catch me, ever!

Ha ha ha ha Ha ha ha!

Now you're getting fancy!

But I'll escape with twinkle toes.

It's a fancy pantsy dancy!

It seems to me an **engineer**
has helped with this design.
Too bad this little Leprechaun
is going to be just fine.

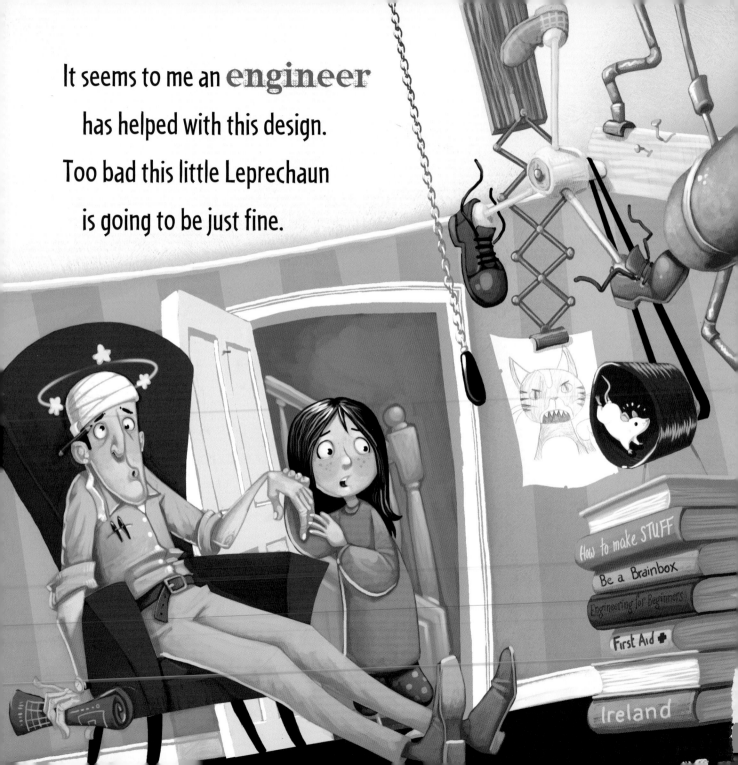

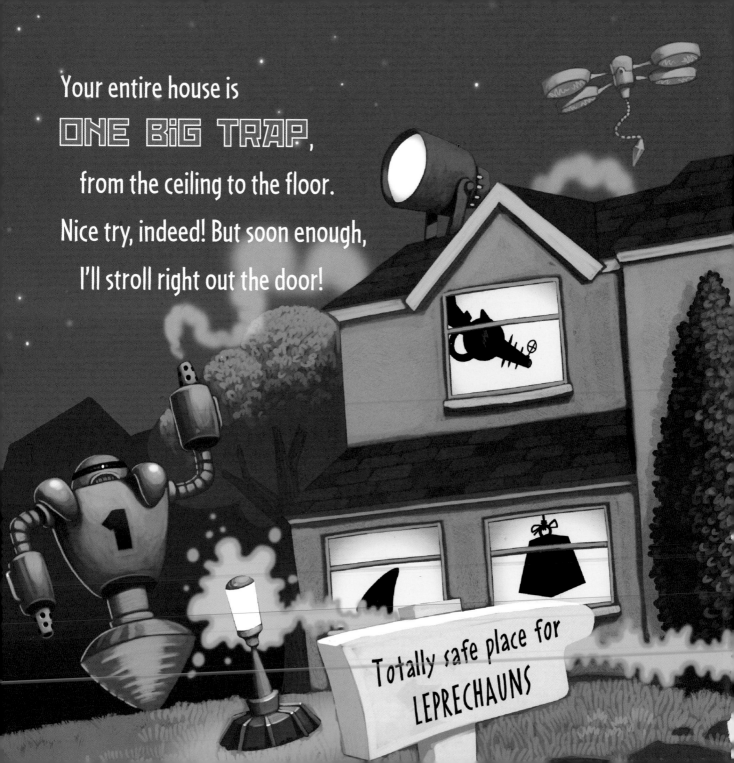

Your entire house is
ONE BIG TRAP,
from the ceiling to the floor.
Nice try, indeed! But soon enough,
I'll stroll right out the door!

Totally safe place for LEPRECHAUNS

The **LEPRECHAUN BE GONE 3000**™
gave me quite a scare.
But without a four-leaf clover,
I won't be caught in there!

You'll never catch this Leprechaun.
Impossible! That's a fact!
Unless, one day, a brilliant child
designs *the*
perfect
trap!

But *who* will that child be?